The
BOO BABY GIRL
Meets
the GHOST of
Mable's Gable

Told by

Jim May

Illustrated by

Shawn Finley

Brotherstone Publishers

Elgin, Illinois

To All my Friends, at Randall School, Enjoy!

Jim May
11/92

(This book given to the Randall School library in Matthew Martin's name - class of 6/92)

Published by
BROTHERSTONE PUBLISHERS
1340 Pleasant Drive, Elgin, IL 60123

Printed in the United States of America

Library of Congress Catalog Card Number: 92-72702

May, Jim
The boo baby girl meets the ghost of
mable's gable/written by Jim May;
illustrated by Shawn Finley.   p.   cm.
Summary: A playful horror tale about two swaggering eighth-
grade boys who are scared off by Mable's ghost and fail to
get the gold and a fearless toddler who is not and does.
ISBN 1-878925-03-2
[1. Ghosts - Fiction. 2. Haunted houses - Fiction.]
I. Finley, Shawn, ill. II. Title.
PZ7.L   Bo 1992   [E]   92-72702

An audio cassette entitled **Heroes, Heroines, and Boo Babies**, featuring "The Boo Baby Girl Meets the Ghost of Mable's Gable" and three more stories told by Jim May, is available from: BELL FARM RECORDINGS, Box 6, Alden, IL 60001 or BROTHERSTONE PUBLISHERS, 1340 Pleasant Drive, Elgin, IL 60123.

Jim May is a professional storyteller. For information about his programs, write to him at Box 1012, Woodstock, IL 60098, or call 815-648-2039.

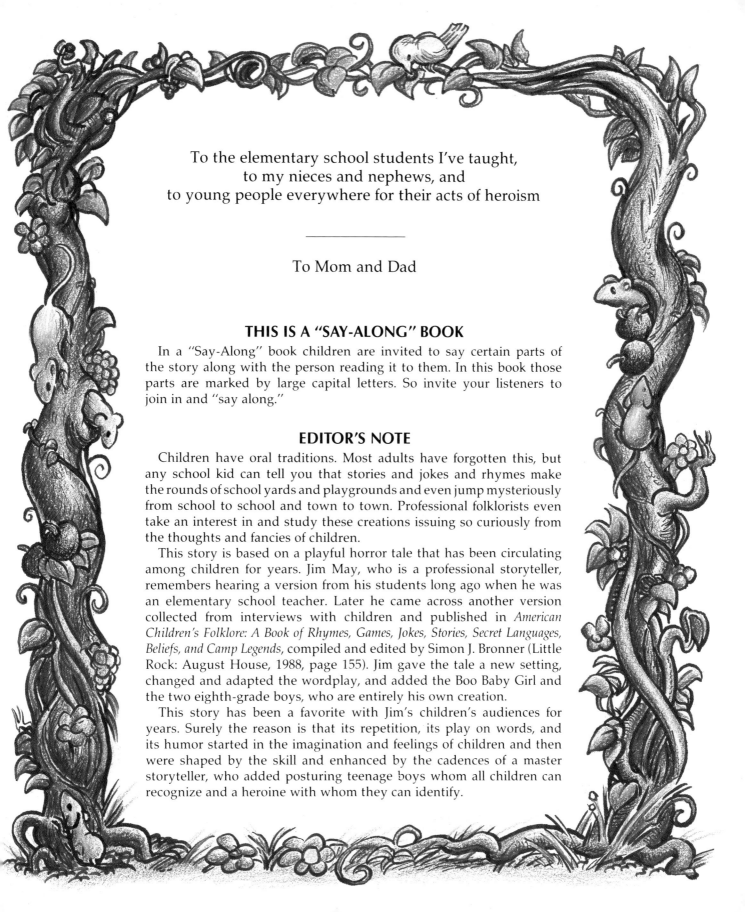

To the elementary school students I've taught,
to my nieces and nephews, and
to young people everywhere for their acts of heroism

———————

To Mom and Dad

THIS IS A "SAY-ALONG" BOOK

In a "Say-Along" book children are invited to say certain parts of the story along with the person reading it to them. In this book those parts are marked by large capital letters. So invite your listeners to join in and "say along."

EDITOR'S NOTE

Children have oral traditions. Most adults have forgotten this, but any school kid can tell you that stories and jokes and rhymes make the rounds of school yards and playgrounds and even jump mysteriously from school to school and town to town. Professional folklorists even take an interest in and study these creations issuing so curiously from the thoughts and fancies of children.

This story is based on a playful horror tale that has been circulating among children for years. Jim May, who is a professional storyteller, remembers hearing a version from his students long ago when he was an elementary school teacher. Later he came across another version collected from interviews with children and published in *American Children's Folklore: A Book of Rhymes, Games, Jokes, Stories, Secret Languages, Beliefs, and Camp Legends*, compiled and edited by Simon J. Bronner (Little Rock: August House, 1988, page 155). Jim gave the tale a new setting, changed and adapted the wordplay, and added the Boo Baby Girl and the two eighth-grade boys, who are entirely his own creation.

This story has been a favorite with Jim's children's audiences for years. Surely the reason is that its repetition, its play on words, and its humor started in the imagination and feelings of children and then were shaped by the skill and enhanced by the cadences of a master storyteller, who added posturing teenage boys whom all children can recognize and a heroine with whom they can identify.

I want to tell you about a friend of mine. I call her the Boo Baby Girl. She's about two years old. She's about two feet tall. She has chubby legs. She wears a diaper. She has that toddler walk— you know—kind of a bowlegged waddle.

Here's the most important part of the story if you want to remember it and tell it to somebody. She went to a nursery school. The school was called the Pied Piper Nursery School. It was named after the story of the Pied Piper of Hamlin. If you know that story and you hear someone say, "The piper must be paid," you'll know what they are talking about.

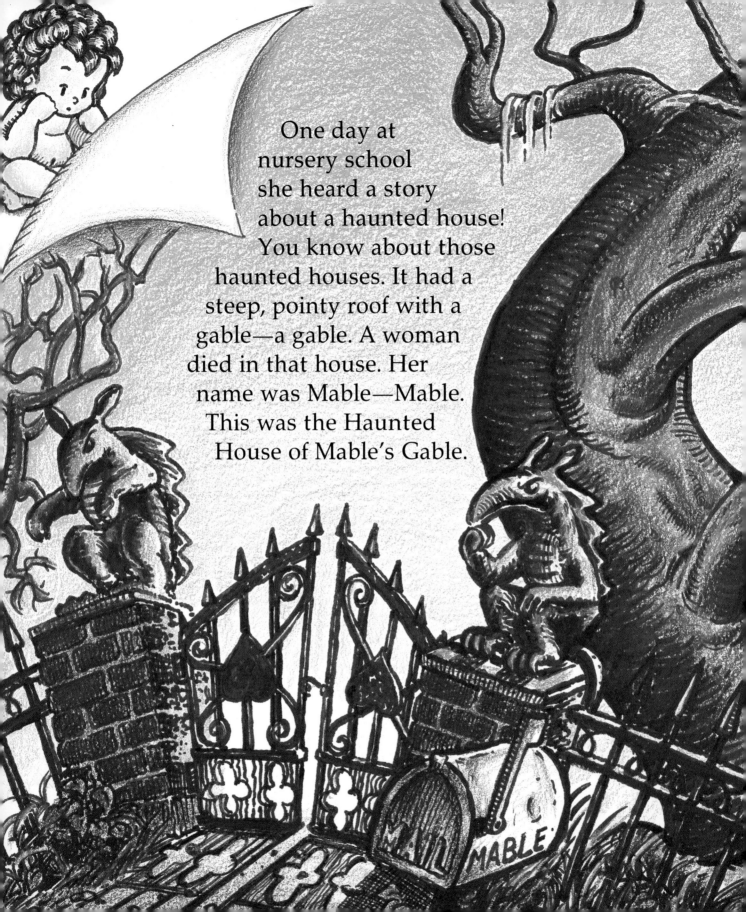

One day at
nursery school
she heard a story
about a haunted house!
You know about those
haunted houses. It had a
steep, pointy roof with a
gable—a gable. A woman
died in that house. Her
name was Mable—Mable.
This was the Haunted
House of Mable's Gable.

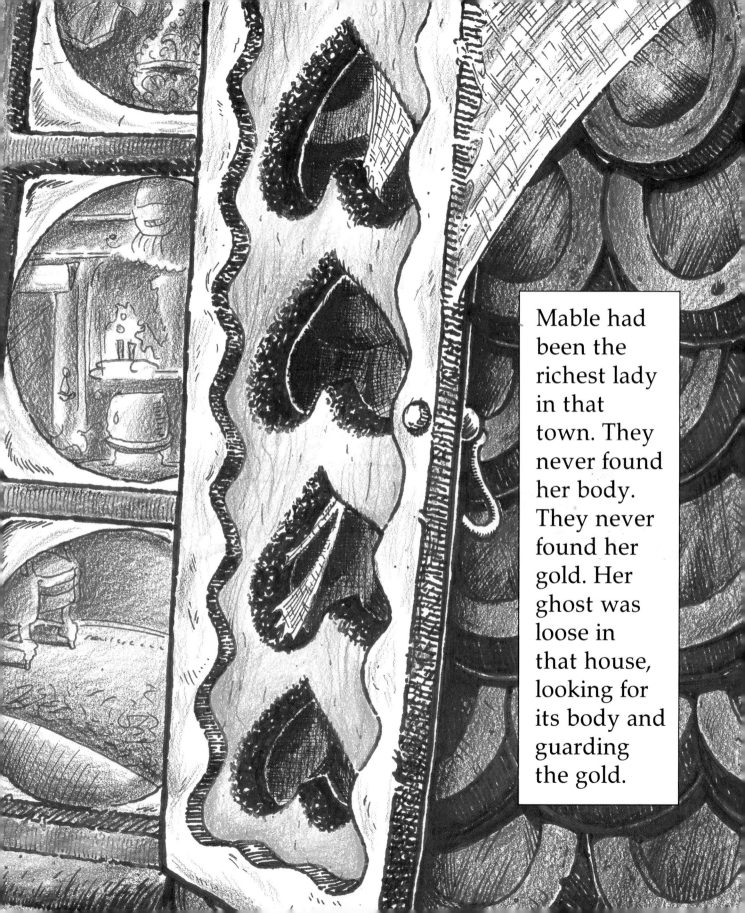

Mable had been the richest lady in that town. They never found her body. They never found her gold. Her ghost was loose in that house, looking for its body and guarding the gold.

Finally two guys decided to get that gold. They weren't afraid of the ghost. They were big guys, tough guys, mean guys—they were eighth grade boys!

They weren't scared when they went to that haunted house.

One of those eighth grade boys stood guard on the porch. He pumped some iron while he watched. Oo-ah, oo-ah, oo-ah.

The other eighth grade boy, a big guy, tough guy, mean guy, opened the door. Eeeeeeek—it squeaked.

He walked down the hallway—tha-thump, tha-thump, tha-thump. And then he saw it! On the big oak table—a bag of gold! He thought of all the things he could buy at the mall! "All right! Gold!"

He grabbed the bag. But when he did, he heard a sound. It came from above him, below him, all around him. It was a voice— a howl, a moan: **"I'M THE GHOST OF MABLE'S GABLE. I SAY THE MONEY STAYS ON THE TABLE!"**

Pshew! He was running out of that room, down the hallway, and out past his friend on the porch like a flash.

His friend, the other eighth grade boy, thought, "What a chicken! I will get the gold and I won't have to split it with him!" You see he was also a big guy, tough guy, mean guy. He opened the door of the haunted house— Eeeeeeek!

He walked down the hallway—tha-thump, tha-thump, tha-thump! And then he saw it too—the bag of gold on the table! He thought to himself, "I'm rich! Hot rods!"

He grabbed that bag of gold, but when he did, he heard the horrible voice: **"I'M THE GHOST OF MABLE'S GABLE. I SAY THE MONEY STAYS ON THE TABLE!"**

Pshew!
He was
out of there,
running down
the hallway and
all the way home
with no gold!

Now the Boo Baby Girl was at nursery school that day. Remember, it was the Pied Piper Nursery School. She heard this story about the gold, the ghost, the two guys, and the whole deal, and she thought to herself, "I-I could go down to that haunted house after school...

...and pick up
some cash!"
And she did.

She hitched up her diaper...

...and walked right down to that haunted house on her chubby legs. She walked up the steps of the porch.

She opened the door— Eeeeeeek! She walked down the hallway— thumpa, thumpa, thumpa, thumpa!

And she saw it too! There on the table— the bag of gold! And she thought to herself, "Bubble gum!"

She grabbed that bag of gold
and heard that horrible voice:
**"I'M THE GHOST OF MABLE'S
GABLE. I SAY THE MONEY
STAYS ON THE TABLE!"**
And the Boo Baby Girl said,
"I-I-I-I'm the baby from Pied Piper . . .

...I say the money **GOES IN MY DIAPER!**" She grabbed the money and walked out of that house with a diaper full of gold.

And that's how the Boo Baby Girl got rich.